AF206957

Teens and DIETING

By Anjali Stenquist

San Diego, CA

For more information, contact:
ReferencePoint Press, Inc.
PO Box 27779
San Diego, CA 92198
www.ReferencePointPress.com

Content Consultant: Jessica L. Luzier, Associate Professor, Department of Behavioral Medicine & Psychiatry, West Virginia University School of Medicine

LIBRARY OF CONGRESS CATALOGING-IN-PUBLICATION DATA

Name: Stenquist, Anjali, 1991– author.
Title: Teens and Dieting / by Anjali Stenquist.
Description: San Diego, CA : ReferencePoint Press, Inc., [2019] | Series: Teen Health and Safety | Audience: Grade 9 to 12. | Includes bibliographical references and index.
Identifiers: LCCN 2018011550 (print) | LCCN 2018012117 (ebook) | ISBN 9781682825068 (ebook) | ISBN 9781682825051 (hardback)
Subjects: LCSH: Eating disorders in adolescence—Juvenile literature. | Weight loss—Juvenile literature. | Teenagers—Nutrition—Juvenile literature.
Classification: LCC RJ506.E18 (ebook) | LCC RJ506.E18 S73 2019 (print) | DDC 616.85/2600835—dc23
LC record available at https://lccn.loc.gov/2018011550

CONTENTS

THE WORLD OF DIETING

Aliya loved gymnastics as a child. But after going through puberty, her body changed and filled out. She felt uncomfortable in her leotard and out of place practicing with her thinner peers. Her coach recommended she try a diet.

The options for dieting were seemingly endless. Each diet promised better health, glowing skin, a lean physique, or more energy for living her "best life." Aliya's friend Neil had used the Atkins diet to lose weight for the wrestling team, so Aliya decided to give it a try.

The diet had Aliya eating a lot of protein and few carbohydrates. She started taking her own lunch to school and passing up pizza at parties. She held on to the image of a thinner version of herself on the balance beam wowing the judges and her team. To get faster results, Aliya started a food journal where she tracked all the food she ate. The compliments came rolling in from her coach and her friends.

After a few weeks, Aliya noticed other changes. She was tired all the time, and she was throwing up outside of class. The school nurse explained she had put her body into a state called *ketosis*, which can have symptoms of fatigue, nausea, and weakness. The nurse recommended she stop dieting immediately.

As soon as Aliya quit her diet, her weight bounced back up.
She tried other diets, but the results were good for only a little while.
Soon the weight came back with interest. It took Aliya a long time
to train herself out of dieting and into listening to her body's natural
cues of hunger and fullness. When she graduated from high school,
she reflected on how much time she had spent obsessing on the
size and shape of her body. She wished she had spent that time on
gymnastics, her favorite classes, or hanging out with friends.

The Dieting Industry

Advertisements on the Internet and television promise the possibility
of losing weight through gym memberships, diet pills, and the latest
weight loss technology. Americans spend approximately $40 billion
every year dieting. Many teenagers have attempted to lose weight at
some point in their lives. Dieting behavior often begins in middle and
high school.

But dieting is not an effective method of weight loss. Dieting even
just once can lead to obsessive dieting and abnormal eating habits
as one failed diet leads to another attempt. Neuroscientist Sandra
Aamodt points out, "If diets worked, we'd all be thin by now. . . .
On average, people who go on a diet end up heavier five years later
than people of the same initial weight who didn't diet."[1]

Dieting erodes the body's ability to communicate feelings of
fullness and hunger. Repeated dieting is linked to heart disease,
stroke, diabetes, and a
compromised immune system.
Dieting can also lead to
life-threatening eating disorders.
Project HEAL, an organization
that helps fund eating disorder
treatment, states, "The reality

**"If diets worked, we'd all
be thin by now."[1]**

– Sandra Aamodt, neuroscientist

is that dieting, no matter its form, is counter to what our bodies are intuitively capable of doing. For individuals who are susceptible to having an eating disorder, dieting can be the trigger that influences the development of these fatal illnesses."[2]

Research published in the medical journal *BMJ* found that teenage girls who diet are five times more likely to develop a serious eating disorder such as bulimia, anorexia, or binge eating disorder. These eating disorders can be deadly. Anorexia is the most frequently fatal psychiatric disease, and every 62 minutes at least one individual dies as a direct result of an eating disorder.

Why Does Dieting Continue to Thrive?

For some people, dieting is a way to exercise control over the body and gain the admiration of others. Megan Jayne Crabbe, an anorexia survivor and advocate of healthy eating habits, wrote about why she dieted on her blog: "I started my first diet when I was 10. . . . I slowly dropped a dress size, and basked in the compliments of my peers. I began to value my iron will. . . . With my eyes locked on the holy grail of thin, my self worth laid bare and exposed, I was hooked."[3]

Historian Joan Jacobs Brumberg offers a further explanation in *The Body Project: An Intimate History of American Girls*. She writes: "In the twentieth century, the body has become the central personal project of American girls."[4] A false message—the idea that to be thin is to be beautiful and healthy—is constantly reinforced. As thinness is demanded in young women, an equally dangerous trend for young men emphasizes a muscular physique, making rates of body dissatisfaction almost equal between young men and women. The use of steroids and other supplements to increase muscle mass is similar to using vomiting and excessive exercise to lose weight. All of these behaviors involve taking extreme actions to achieve a particular body image.

A Healthy Lifestyle

The falsehood at the heart of diet culture says that weight loss can be achieved quickly, safely, and permanently. Historian Louise Foxcroft asserts, "We need to re-think our quest for unrealistic thinness through sometimes dangerous, expensive and misguided crash diets and pills, and return to a simple, sensible healthy approach to eating."[5] Research out of the University of Manitoba confirms that individuals should "focus on health rather than weight. By encouraging physical activity and healthy nutrition among all individuals, everyone, regardless of weight status, may benefit with respect to health and well-being."[6]

Dietary supplements are not regulated in the same way as regular foods and drug products. Studies of the health impacts of dietary supplements mostly look at adults and not teenagers.

Once dieting becomes a part of everyday life, it can be very hard for people to regain healthy eating behavior. However, understanding the science behind dieting can help teens make positive choices about their bodies. Placing body image in its cultural context can help them achieve body acceptance at any weight. Understanding the dangerous side effects of dieting can also help teens avoid starting down the dieting cycle. Finally, recognizing what healthy eating behaviors look like can help teens achieve a healthy and empowered lifestyle.

WHAT IS DIETING?

The American Academy of Pediatrics defines dieting as "caloric restriction with the goal of weight loss."[7] People are dieting anytime they eat less to change the way their bodies look. Increasingly, dieting is a major issue facing young people: up to two-thirds of teenage girls and one-third of teenage boys have attempted to lose weight. Before attempting any dieting behavior, it is important that teens understand what dieting is and how it has become a common practice.

Basic Concepts of Nutrition

Dieting is based on principles of nutrition, the interaction of substances in food that can promote the health of an organism. The nutrients required for human health are separated into macronutrients, which are needed in large amounts, and micronutrients, which are needed in small amounts. Micronutrients include vitamins and minerals. Macronutrients include carbohydrates, fats, and proteins. Specific diets for weight loss or muscle growth often restrict one macronutrient and prioritize another. For example, Aliya's Atkins diet restricted her intake of carbohydrates and encouraged her intake of proteins.

Carbohydrates provide energy to the body. Simple carbohydrates, such as those found in candy and soft drinks, can be rapidly absorbed into the bloodstream and cause blood sugar levels to spike. High blood sugar can lead to diseases such as diabetes. Complex carbohydrates require more time to digest. These carbs include green vegetables, whole grains, legumes, and starches such as potatoes. During digestion, the body breaks complex carbs down into simple carbs. Because the process takes longer, blood sugar levels remain in a normal range. Once carbohydrates are broken down into simple sugars, the body can use them for energy.

Fats serve as an energy reserve in the body and also protect vital organs. While fats are necessary for the body to function properly, some fats are healthier than others. Saturated fats are solid at room temperature. They include butter and the fat inside or around meat. Too much saturated fat in a diet has been associated with poor health consequences. Unsaturated fats are typically liquid at room temperature. They include oils and mostly come from plant sources, such as nuts or seeds. Fish also contains unsaturated fats. These fats are associated with better health.

Proteins are a crucial component of skin, blood, bones, and muscles. They are found in every cell of the human body, and they are necessary for repairing damaged tissues. The body does not store protein, so people need to make sure they get enough protein each day. Proteins are found in animal products such as meat, fish, and eggs, but they can also be found in legumes, nuts, and beans.

All of these macronutrients are crucial to the health and proper functioning of the human body. When people diet by cutting out one nutrient or focusing heavily on another, they can overwhelm the delicate balance of nutrition required by the body. When the body does not get enough of one kind of nutrient, or when it receives more of a nutrient than it can handle, the result is often disease.

A Short History of Dieting

Men and women have been experimenting with diets for centuries. Almost one thousand years ago, after he took control of much of France and all of England, William the Conqueror went on to develop the first diet in recorded history. Modern historians believe he may have suffered from a medical condition that caused him to gain weight on an already unusually large frame. When he could no longer ride a horse, William decided to lie in his bed and consume only liquids. He believed this would be the key to losing his extra bulk. William found little success with his plan. But his efforts to reduce his size by ignoring his hunger and allowing minimal food into his body would be repeated by many.

One of the first diets to gain a large following was developed by an English undertaker named William Banting in 1863. After losing a significant amount of weight, Banting wrote a pamphlet called *Letter on Corpulence, Addressed to the Public.* The pamphlet explained how Banting lost his obesity by avoiding sugar, starch, beer, milk, and butter. Banting's ideas were not new, but his writing became so popular that people used *Banting* as slang for *dieting* years after the publication of his pamphlet.

Counting calories became a fad at the turn of the twentieth century with the publication of the 1915 bestselling book *How to Live* by Irving Fisher and Dr. Eugene Lyman Fisk. Fisher and Fisk believed that the only way to truly control one's weight was to focus not just on the amount or type of food consumed, but also on the number of calories in it.

A calorie is a unit of energy. It refers to how much energy the body absorbs from a given amount of food. In *How to Live*, Fisk and Fisher wrote, "Nature counts every calorie very carefully. If the number of calories taken in exceeds the number used by the body (or excreted

William the Conqueror was duke of Normandy and later king of England in the eleventh century. He is credited with creating the first diet.

unused), the excess accumulates in fat or tissue."[8] This idea—that all calories not burned in exercise would become fat tissue—caught on like wildfire. While the body does store excess calories as fat, the assumption that eating fewer calories will result in weight loss is grossly simplistic. Yet many followed Fisk and Fisher's model for weight loss, including writer Lulu Hunt Peters. Her influential 1918 book *Diet and Health with Key to the Calories* began a craze of calorie counting in the United States. The book's success prompted high-end restaurants to begin including calories on their menus.

Even as the economic collapse of the Great Depression brought crippling poverty and hunger to the United States in the 1930s, an obsession with counting calories sank deep into the American mindset. Peters falsely insisted in her newspaper columns in the 1920s that 75 percent of Americans were "seriously overweight."[9] Health concerns around obesity do drive many healthy weight loss goals. But creating panic around obesity in the United States has also been used to sell diet books for almost one hundred years.

Physical Changes in the Average American

One hundred years ago, individuals experienced more widespread malnutrition, higher risk of disease, and a very different set of physical demands placed on their bodies. Their average life expectancy was shorter. Because of increased strain on the body, the onset of puberty came much later in their lives.

In the 1960s, a study of military draft records revealed that the average man was ten pounds heavier than his counterpart during the Civil War (1861–1865). Gradual improvement in health and increase in weight has been a sign of progress in the United States as disease rates, food scarcity, and health risks to workers decreased. However, a more dramatic change in the past forty years has caused alarm over an "obesity epidemic" in which "38 percent of U.S. adults are obese and 17 percent of teenagers are [obese]," according to reports from the Centers for Disease Control and Prevention.[10]

According to the US Department of Agriculture, the average American ate 2,234 calories per day in 1970 and 2,757 per day in 2003. That is an increase of 23 percent. More than half of those extra calories came from fats, oils, sugar, and sweeteners. Sugar and sweeteners are high in calories, but that is not their only impact on the body. When they enter the bloodstream, they trigger the release of insulin, which begins to quickly convert the food that cannot be immediately used by the body into stored fat. Added sugars have been linked to depression, chronic inflammation, diabetes, arthritis, obesity, heart disease, and even cancer.

In his 2009 book *The End of Overeating,* former head of the US Food and Drug Administration Dr. David Kessler claimed the American food industry has created addicts to high-sugar, high-fat, and high-salt foods. Kessler argued that the human brain responds to these foods with the same pleasure response released by morphine and heroin. This pleasure response is the release of hormones called *endorphins*, which are typically released in response to pain, vigorous exercise, and laughter. A release of endorphins limits feelings of pain and fosters feelings of pleasure and euphoria. Researchers believe addiction to drugs such as morphine and heroin is caused by a release of endorphins. Kessler believed certain processed foods could have the same addictive effect as drugs by causing the brain to release endorphins.

As the American diet becomes larger and less nutritious, Americans are also becoming much less physically active. From 1988 to 2010, the proportion of Americans reporting very low rates of physical activity rose from 19 to 52 percent in women and from 11 to 43 percent in men. Part of this lifestyle change may be due to the popularity of sedentary entertainment. The Henry J. Kaiser Family Foundation studied media usage in young people. In 2009, eight- to eighteen-year-olds spent an average of 7.5 hours per day with

Video games and other media are considered sedentary entertainment. They may have contributed to changes in weight for the average American.

computers, video games, and television. As a result, only one-third of high school students get the levels of physical activity recommended by medical professionals. Along with changes in food intake, changes in activity levels have contributed to a dramatic increase in the weight of the average American in the last forty years.

Economics of Obesity

Between 2003 and 2007, obesity increased by approximately 10 percent for all US children. For children in low-education and low-income households, the increase was closer to 30 percent. A 2006 study published in the *Journal of the American Academy of Pediatrics* looked at one of the causes of this disparity. The study compared neighborhoods of low-income and minority residents with nonminority and higher socioeconomic neighborhoods. The study found there were significantly fewer safe places where low-income and minority children could be physically active, such as public parks and community centers. Access to these neighborhood facilities leads to a significantly smaller risk of obesity in children.

Access to supermarkets and convenience stores where healthy food can be purchased is also more limited in low socioeconomic, minority, and rural neighborhoods. The term *food desert* has been coined to describe areas where fresh fruits, vegetables, and other healthful options are unavailable. A study published in the *American Journal of Preventative Medicine* in 2008 further found that "the availability of fast-food restaurants and energy-dense foods has been found to be greater in lower-income and minority neighborhoods."[11] The lack of access to healthy food and increased access to heavily processed food factor heavily into rates of obesity.

Obesity affects Americans at all socioeconomic levels, but it disproportionately affects individuals living in a lower socioeconomic bracket. Yale University professor Kelly D. Brownell wrote in the *LA Times*, "The reality stares us in the face - poverty discourages physical activity and encourages excess calorie consumption. Anything but sky-high rates of obesity, diabetes and other diseases would be surprising."[12] Increased rates of obesity lead to devastating health consequences more frequently affecting lower socioeconomic and minority communities.

Health Consequences of Obesity

The World Health Organization defines obesity and the condition of being overweight as "abnormal or excessive fat accumulation that may impair health."[13] There are different types of obesity, and each of them has different health outcomes. To understand obesity and its negative health consequences, it is important to first examine the role of fat in the body.

All human bodies contain fat. Fat tissue is necessary for protection, cushion, warmth, energy, and the ability to think. The human brain is primarily made of fat. Human cell membranes require fat to function. Fatty acids are essential for life and play key roles in the functioning of the liver, immune system, and hormone regulation. Fat is neither always good nor always bad. It is simply a part of the body.

The body uses fat to store energy. When the body consumes food, the liver transforms carbohydrates and proteins into fat tissue and sends them to different parts of the body for storage. Reservoirs of fat are known as adipose tissue. Adipose tissue is located beneath the skin, around internal organs, in bone marrow, between muscle, and within breast tissue. Not all excess adipose tissue poses the same health risks.

But adipose tissue inside the abdominal cavity is unique. There, adipose tissue becomes semifluid. This type of adipose tissue is known as visceral fat. A buildup of visceral fat leads to a type of obesity known as *central obesity* and has serious health effects. Excess visceral fat is believed to be particularly dangerous because it leads to fat accumulation in the pancreas, heart, and other organs. This can eventually cause lipotoxicity, organ dysfunction associated with type 2 diabetes and heart failure.

Overweight conditions and obesity are measured in body mass index (BMI), a ratio of weight over height meant to indicate if the body is storing excess fat. Overweight is typically categorized between 25.0 and 29.9, while obesity is categorized as 30.0 or higher. BMI calculation can be misleading, however. High-powered athletes often score as overweight because the index does not consider the difference between weight caused by fat and weight caused by muscle.

It is also possible to have a high BMI and still be metabolically healthy. Metabolic health looks at measures such as blood pressure, cholesterol levels, and blood sugar levels. If a person has normal lab tests, they can be obese and metabolically healthy. Doctors also look at a person's waist size: a waist size of under 40 inches (102 cm) for men and 35 inches (89 cm) for women, along with the previous factors, could indicate the person is healthy. This type of obesity is not very common, but it has very different health implications from other types of obesity, such as central obesity.

In general, as BMI increases so do the health risks of diabetes, heart disease, stroke, certain cancers, poor sexual and reproductive health, impacted lung function, and stress to bones, muscles, and joints. The fact that these risks decrease when a person's BMI falls within a lower range does not mean thinner is healthier. For a body to function, a certain amount of fat tissue is needed. Where that fat tissue is stored and how it looks is different for each body. Waist-to-hip ratio, normal blood sugar, and an active lifestyle are far better indications of good health than BMI.

Can Dieting Work?

Concern about the health consequences of being overweight has led many Americans to diet. But according to the research, diets do not work. In one study conducted by the magazine *Consumer Reports*, 25 percent of dieters successfully kept off 10 percent of their body

> **"[A]ll experts agree that the long-term success rate for weight loss is bad; the only question is how bad."[14]**
>
> – Sandra Aamodt, neuroscientist

weight for at least one year. However, most dieters seek to lose more weight than that and for a longer period of time. Researcher Sandra Aamodt asserts "all experts agree that the long-term success rate for weight loss is bad; the only question is how bad."[14]

Even the diet industry knows dieting does not work in the long run for most people. Datamonitor, a market research company that analyzes the dieting industry, noted in its 2003 report, "In 2002, 231 million Europeans attempted some form of diet. Of these only 1% will achieve permanent weight loss."[15] Weight Watchers, a popular weight loss program, conducted its own research. It found the average weight loss in any dieting program is roughly a 5 percent reduction of body weight in six months, with a return of at least a third of the weight after two years. As an example, a young woman weighing 140 pounds (64 kg) might lose approximately 7 pounds (3 kg) over six months. She would likely gain more than 2 pounds (1 kg) back within the next two years.

In fact, in the long run, dieting strongly predicts future weight gain. On television and in advertising, weight loss experts repeat Fisk and Fisher's simple equation, encouraging dieters to burn more calories than they take in to lose weight. However, much more is at play when people take in and burn calories.

Bodies Do Not Want to Lose Weight

For most of human history, access to food has been unpredictable. For early humans, medieval farmers, or Americans living through the Great Depression, alternating times of famine and feast meant a frequent fear of starvation. While gaining weight can have negative health consequences, the risk of death by starvation is much worse. As a result, the human body has developed incredible methods of surviving periods in which food is scarce. Though dieting may be a conscious choice, the body understands periods of dieting as periods of starvation, and it uses all of its tools to keep itself from starving.

Defended Weight and Set Point

The body has a range of approximately 10–15 pounds (5–7 kg) that the brain believes is its normal weight. This range is different for each individual and is generally referred to as the *defended weight*. The brain has two goals related to defended weight: that it should remain stable and that it should not decrease too much.

Both of these goals make sense when put into the context of human history, but that second goal can become problematic for someone trying to lose weight. Defended weight rises fairly easily, and some research shows that defended weight increases gradually with age. Defended weight is difficult to lower, even if a person has already spent years at a lower weight. According to the Massachusetts Institute of Technology (MIT) Medical Center, "body fat percentage and body weight are matters of internal controls that are set differently in different people."[16] When people diet, they engage in a constant battle with this control system, a system determined to keep the body at its defended weight.

How Does the Body Regulate Weight?

Defended weight is like a room with a thermostat set at a particular temperature. If someone in the room opens a window and lets in cold air, the temperature will momentarily go down. But the thermostat makes adjustments and increases the heat in the room to account for the cold air. When a person goes on a diet, they might experience initial quick results, but their efforts are often overpowered by the thermostat-like actions of the brain.

One tool brains employ is a hormone called leptin. Hormones are chemicals the body uses to communicate with itself. Leptin is produced in fat cells. It signals to the brain how much energy is stored in the body as fat. When there is enough fat to be in the defended weight range, leptin signals the reward center of the brain to make eating less enjoyable, naturally preventing weight gain.

When fat stores are lost through dieting, there is no leptin to signal the reward center of the brain. As a result, the brain sends out reward signals around eating, hoping the extra messages about how good it would feel to eat will help the person seek out food and restore the supply of fat in the body. Hunger is another signal that a person needs more calories to restore weight. Because of leptin's absence while dieting, the desire to eat can become overwhelming. This can lead to someone either breaking the diet or obsessing over the idea of food. There is even some evidence that the reward center's response for all things go up when leptin is not around, making people more susceptible to addiction and other risky behavior while dieting.

Metabolism is another tool the body uses to keep weight within the defended range. Metabolism is the process of converting food into energy. The body will speed up the process of metabolism if weight is gained in order to use up extra calories. It will slow down metabolism if weight is lost. As the MIT Medical Center states, the brain "is very good at supervising fat storage, but it cannot tell the difference between dieting and starvation." When dieters deprive their bodies of calories, their bodies respond by slowing down metabolism. Dieters feel tired and depressed, and their bodies burn calories at a slower rate. The MIT Medical Center goes on to state, "After an initial, relatively quick loss, dieters often become stuck at a plateau and then lose weight at a much slower rate, although they remain as hungry as ever."[17] Once dieters hit that plateau, further weight loss can be extremely difficult to achieve.

Can Dieting Lead to Weight Gain?

Researchers in Finland conducted a nine-year study on dieting. The study focused on sets of twins so that genetics and the environment would be as similar as possible between the people in the study. Only one twin in each set dieted. At the end of the study, the twin who dieted was more likely to have gained weight. The study concluded that going on a diet once increased the odds of men becoming overweight by a factor of two and women by a factor of three. Women who went on two or more diets were five times as likely to become overweight by the age of twenty-five.

The reason may lie in the brain's belief that dieting is a state of famine. Once the famine is over, the brain takes precautions to keep the body healthy in case it is faced with famine again. These precautions include increasing the amount of energy stored as fat.

Caloric restriction is a very stressful event for bodies. The primary stress hormone cortisol is vital in regulating blood sugar, metabolism, and salt levels. However, during periods of immediate or long-term stress, cortisol slows down the functions of the body that are not critical. These noncritical functions include the digestive system, reproductive system, and growth process. The slowing down of the digestive system can lead to increased abdominal fat. In this way, an increase in cortisol levels has been strongly linked with obesity and weight gain. The stressful act of dieting counterproductively encourages the body to slow down its digestion and store fat.

Dieting also fundamentally changes the way hunger is understood. Rather than following the intuitive clues to eat when hungry and stop when full, dieters follow external clues—eating a certain number of calories at certain times. Dieting can slowly cause dieters to experience a loss of connection to internal cues of hunger and satisfaction, leading to binge eating or emotional eating down the road.

Poor body image often leads people to dieting in order to change the way they look. Body image is subjective and is closely tied with a person's self-esteem and self-acceptance.

Why Do People Continue to Diet?

Many people who are not overweight are still motivated to diet. Half of the women who reported being on a diet between 2003 and 2008 were considered to be at or even below normal weight. A big reason lies in body perception. The National Eating Disorder Association (NEDA) defines body image as "how you see yourself when you look in the mirror or picture yourself in your mind."[18] Body image plays a crucial role in affecting how people relate to beauty standards and whether they choose to diet.

Chapter 2

WHY DO TEENS DIET?

In a 2011 interview with National Public Radio, actress Mindy Kaling referred to dieting as "an American pastime."[19] The Boston Medical Center estimates that 45 million Americans are on a diet. Between 2003 and 2008, 57 percent of American women and 40 percent of American men reported being on a diet at some point during the previous year. Dieting culture starts young. By the age of thirteen, 53 percent of American girls are unsatisfied with the way their bodies look. By the age of seventeen, the number rises to 78 percent. Reports now indicate that rates of body dissatisfaction are equal in adolescent boys as well.

As bodies naturally change during puberty, a desire to remain thin or to instantly build up muscle mass can devastate rates of body satisfaction and drive preteens to dieting. Many preteens and teenagers are already at a normal weight when they begin dieting. The reasons for the widespread desire to be thinner, more muscular, or differently proportioned are complex. In the research journal *Paediatrics & Child Health*, researchers wrote, "In addition to being exposed to the very real health risks of obesity and poor nutrition, teenagers are being exposed to the unrealistically thin beauty idea that is portrayed in the media."[20] Changing beauty standards contribute to teenagers' feelings of body dissatisfaction and to dieting culture.

Standards of Beauty

Beauty is a cultural idea. It refers to whatever physical appearance is valued at a particular time and place. For instance, Marie de'Medici was a queen of France in the early seventeenth century. A great patron of the arts, she was considered a beautiful woman in particular for her rounded neck. It is a curious point of fashion that for a brief period of time having a medical condition that caused the thyroid to swell was considered the peak of beauty. A stroll through an art museum reveals the many different standards of beauty that have been in place throughout human history.

Beauty standards contribute to America's enormous dieting culture. From Captain America action figures to airbrushed Victoria's Secret models, the gulf between the average American body and the bodies held up as examples of beauty seems to grow ever wider. People may begin to think of themselves using hurtful labels, such as fat or skinny, and not within their valuable roles, such as dancer, athlete, student, or friend. They may become vulnerable to believing that their bodies are problems to be solved, rather than part of a rich, multifaceted life. When seeking to solve these perceived problems of the body, individuals often turn to dieting.

In American history, cultural standards of beauty have driven men and women to take dramatic and unhealthy measures to change their appearances. Dieting in order to achieve thinness or muscle tone is one such unhealthy measure. The Body Project at Bradley University urges young people to ask the following critical questions: "Why is the American body ideal for women so thin today? And why is the body ideal for men so large and muscular? Does this tell us anything about the roles we expect men and women to fulfill?"[21]

The Perfect Girl

One of the first female American beauty icons was "the Gibson Girl." Drawn by artist Charles Dana Gibson in the late 1800s, the Gibson Girl was the ideal young woman. She was tall and thin with exaggerated hips and breasts held in place by a swan-bill corset that forced the torso forward and made the wearer's hips jut out in back. There were many characteristics associated with the Gibson Girl, but her physical figure inspired a generation of young women to emulate her dramatic curves with corsets that caused significant damage to the spine. The first "perfect" American body required effort, pain, and money to maintain, but it was only in fashion for a brief period before another body type replaced the Gibson Girl.

In the 1920s, the flapper took on the role of the perfect body. Unlike the Gibson Girl, the flapper had a boyish figure devoid of curves and did not wear a corset. From a beauty ideal that required exaggerated hips and breasts, the new ideal prized thinness. American women were asked to change their bodies to fit a very different silhouette in a pattern of constantly changing beauty standards that continues today. Instead of requiring women to wear restrictive corsets to hold their bodies in particular shapes, the new beauty ideal required women to change the shapes of their bodies themselves.

The rise in popularity of the flapper, combined with the practice of calorie counting made popular by Lulu Hunt Peters, introduced an obsession with weight and dieting as part of American culture. This marked the beginning of diet culture in the United States and was a direct response to the new beauty ideal. In *Never Satisfied: A Cultural History of Diets, Fantasies and Fat*, Hillel Schwartz argues that weight became the focus of varied industries. In law enforcement, detectives and officers began noting suspects' weight as a measure of their characters, equating more weight with a poorer character. In health care, life insurance companies began judging a person's mortality based on his or her weight. Dieting became a way for people to prove themselves to be fit, fashionable, and morally upright. Schwartz states,

> *The penny public scale, the bathroom scale and the kitchen food scale were instruments by which the narrowing tolerances for the healthy body were given force and a substantial numerical presence. The Roaring Twenties were also the calculating, calorie-controlled, self-conscious Grim Twenties.*[22]

People have been chasing beauty standards for hundreds of years. The Gibson Girl was the standard of female beauty during the late 1800s and early 1900s.

Just as the standard for the perfect American body has changed from decade to decade, the attitudes of young people toward the standards of beauty have shifted as well. Historian Joan Jacobs Brumberg collected the diaries of young women between 1890 and the 1990s in her book *The Body Project: An Intimate History of American Girls.* In her book, Brumberg draws a comparison between the New Year's resolutions of two girls living one hundred years apart. The diarist in 1892 wrote that her goals were "not to talk about [her] self or feelings. To think before speaking. To work seriously. To be self restrained in conversation and actions. Not to let [her] thoughts wander. To be dignified. Interest [her]self more in others."[23] The more modern young girl wrote the following in the 1990s: "I will try to make myself better in any way I possibly can with the help of my budget and baby-sitting money. I will lose weight, get new lenses, already got a new haircut, good makeup, new clothes and accessories."[24]

This shift toward fitting a standard of beauty rather than a set of admired characteristics is part of a greater trend Brumberg observed in the diaries. As the diaries got closer to the present day, the attitudes of their authors toward their bodies became more like generals commanding unruly armies. Their bodies became something to be managed and maintained. By the 1990s, Brumberg observed the diarists wrote most often about relationships and body insecurity.

According to NEDA and the Centers for Disease Control and Prevention, girls today begin to talk about body image anxiety around the age of six. Roughly half of elementary school girls are concerned about their weight or about becoming too fat. As girls grow older, their body satisfaction continues to lower, along with their levels of self-esteem. Writer Roxane Gay wrote poignantly in her 2017 memoir *Hunger,* "It is a powerful lie to equate thinness with self-worth. Clearly, this lie is convincing because the weight loss industry thrives."[25]

The Barbie doll was introduced into American culture in 1959. Since then, the Barbie doll has gone on to inspire beauty standards for more than half a century.

A study at the University of Sussex looked for the cause of female body dissatisfaction in the toys young girls are given. The researchers found an alarming trend. More than 160 girls between the ages of five and eight were given dolls. Some received Barbie dolls. Others received Emme dolls, which model an adult dress size 16. A control group received no dolls. The young girls given Barbie dolls reported a greater desire for thinness and higher body dissatisfaction.

The Barbie doll is an iconic image of a very particular standard of female beauty. In the 1960s, the company behind Barbie, Mattel, created a "slumber party Barbie" that came with a scale reading

110 pounds (50 kg) and a small book titled *How to Lose Weight*. In 2008, three Barbie dolls were sold every second. In 1995, the Yale Center for Eating and Weight Disorders calculated what a real-world woman would look like if she had the same proportions as a Barbie doll. The center found that the average woman would have had to grow 2 feet (0.6 m) taller, extend her neck by 3.2 inches (8 cm), gain 5 inches (13 cm) in chest size, and lose 6 inches (15 cm) around her waist in order to emulate Barbie's proportions. A life-sized Barbie would be incapable of lifting her head, would have room for only half a liver and a few inches of intestine in her abdominal cavity, and would need to walk on all fours due to having a child's size-three foot.

After enormous backlash against dolls that instill such impossible beauty standards in impressionable children, Mattel announced a new line of Barbies in 2016 that featured different body sizes and shapes. The cover of *Time* magazine's February 2016 issue ran a picture of Barbie's new, more realistic silhouette. Barbie's changing appearance represents women's frustration with strict beauty standards. As the *Time* headline asked, "Now Can We Stop Talking About My Body?"[26]

The Perfect Boy

Though the majority of body scrutiny has historically been aimed at women, more and more focus on male beauty standards has made body insecurity common among young boys and men, too. Dr. Raymond Lemberg, an expert on male eating disorders, was quoted in the *Atlantic* magazine in 2014 as saying, "We used to really discriminate—and we still do—against women. . . . The media has become more of an

> **"It is a powerful lie to equate thinness with self-worth. Clearly, this lie is convincing because the weight loss industry thrives."[25]**
>
> – Roxane Gay, author of *Hunger*

Male superheroes promote a standard of masculinity that demands defined muscles and high stature. This body type is difficult to achieve for most of the population.

equal opportunity discriminator. Men's bodies are not good enough anymore either."[27]

Action figures produced for young boys portray exaggerated muscle mass and little to no fat, a body type reflected in only approximately 1 to 2 percent of the population. These toys impress upon children notions of how the ideal male body should look. Boys are set up to find their own bodies lacking when they inevitably fail to develop in the same way. These feelings of insecurity lead young men to potentially dangerous behaviors, including protein-heavy diets that can wreak havoc on kidney function, protein powders that can contain unregulated ingredients, and steroid use that can have catastrophic and lasting effects on an adolescent body.

The myth that muscularity equals masculinity has compelled up to 4 million Americans to use steroids at some point in their lives. The majority of the individuals using steroids are not athletes but men hoping to change their physical appearance. Risks of premature death, harm to the brain, and heart damage leading to strokes or heart attacks come with any experimentation with steroids.

According to Dr. Lemberg, for every four cases of an eating disorder in the United States, one will impact a male patient. The drive to extreme dieting and other dangerous behavior is not always simply a wish to be thin. It can also be a desire to achieve a more muscular physique. Both desires can end in equally damaging and life-threatening outcomes.

Media Pressure vs. Reality

While it is unclear why exactly children are feeling more intense pressure for their bodies to be thin or more muscular, some researchers believe it may be linked to the rise in the overall weight of the American population and a lack of representation in media. Despite the changing body size of the American public, individuals who fit the thin beauty standard are overwhelmingly featured in television and advertising.

In 2000, only 24 percent of male actors and 13 percent of female actors featured on prime-time television shows were overweight, compared with a general population in which 60 percent of men and 50 percent of women were overweight. Research conducted at the University of Sussex found that exposing young women to ultra-thin or average-sized models lowered both body satisfaction and self-esteem. An unrepresentative portrayal of American bodies has likely contributed to the obsession with dieting.

One area of media that does feature overweight and obese individuals is reality television. *The Biggest Loser* went on air for the first time in 2004 and was broadcast for thirteen years. *The Biggest Loser* chronicles the stories of overweight and obese contestants attempting to win a cash prize for losing the most weight. During its most popular season, the show reached more than 10 million viewers. Though taken off the air, the legacy of the program lives on in spin-offs and related shows such as *Extreme Makeover: Weight Loss*, *Fit to Fat to Fit*, *My 600-lb Life*, and *Revenge Body*. Some of the only places in media where obese Americans can see their body types reflected are shows that demand that their bodies change.

In 2016, the producers of *The Biggest Loser* were accused of employing dangerous tactics to create more dramatic weight loss. Allegations of forced dehydration, severely restricted caloric intake, and encouraged use of weight-loss drugs have been brought against the show. Such extreme tactics not only put the health of contestants in jeopardy, but, according to a medical study of one season's participants, also slowed the metabolism of thirteen out of fourteen contestants even after the season ended. This slowed metabolism caused contestants to regain the majority of the weight they lost during the show. In some cases, the contestants gained even more weight than they had upon entering the show.

Media portrayal of dramatic weight loss, such as in *The Biggest Loser* and *Revenge Body*, promotes the false narrative that it is possible to safely lose a large amount of weight in a short time and keep it off. Dr. Michael Rosenbaum, an obesity researcher at

Columbia University, responded to the television shows in a *New York Times* article, saying, "the difficulty in keeping weight off reflects biology, not a pathological lack of willpower affecting two-thirds of the U.S.A."[28] Yet the pressure to lose more weight in shorter periods of time persists, even more intimately in social media.

#Fitspo

Thinspiration and fitspiration have entered social media speak as subtle nods toward a very specific beauty ideal that has the potential

HEALTHY VS. THIN

Karime Blanco was a high school junior when she wrote an article for *National Public Radio* on the food she saw her family and peer group eating. In her article, she discussed how her family members felt pressured to change their diet. Her brother's desire to one day make it as a singer fueled his desire to be thin. "To be famous is to be fit," he said. Karime's sister was more concerned about health. Her sister said, "I started noticing that I would wake up in the middle of the night and my arm would be all tingly. . . . I stopped drinking soda and it went away, I think I had pre-diabetes." But Karime also noted that in popular culture "healthy" seemed to be a code word for "thin." Karime pointed out teen magazines that advocated for healthy eating right next to images of rail-thin models. Karime interviewed a nutrition counselor at the University of California, Berkeley, who said teens might not be making the healthy food choices they think they are. According to the nutrition counselor, "Instead of adequately nourishing their bodies, [teens are] cutting down on the amount of food in terms of caloric intake. . . . Low calorie diets don't provide adequate nourishment."

Karime Blanco, "For Teens, 'Healthy' and 'Diet' Aren't the Same," *National Public Radio,* November 16, 2006. www.npr.org.

to negatively impact body image and self-esteem. Thinspiration and fitspiration posts on social media take body shaming from a television set with an off switch to the screen of a smartphone never far away from its owner. Some researchers theorize that thin-ideal representations on new media may even be more powerful than those on traditional media.

Researchers Marika Tiggemann and Mia Zaccardo conducted a study of this social media impact on 130 female undergraduate students. Students were either shown fitspiration images—images meant to inspire exercise and healthy eating—or control images featuring travel. Exposure to the fitspiration images led to "increased negative mood and body dissatisfaction and decreased . . . appearance self-esteem relative to travel images."[29] Tiggemann and Zaccardo found that despite their intention of promoting health, fitspiration posts decrease healthy body image and self-esteem and, simply put, make people unhappy.

Dr. Jennifer Lewallen and Dr. Elizabeth Behm-Morawitz published research out of the University of Missouri on the impact of social media conversations around goals of fitness and body size. Lewallen and Behm-Morawitz found that individuals who followed more fitness boards on Pinterest were more likely to engage in extreme weight loss behavior. The researchers wrote,

> *The examination of the influence of thin-ideal or fit-ideal images in a social media context is particularly important in an increasingly globalized world. Women, educators, and users of social media may be informed by this research and consider ways to educate young girls and women to engage with social media critically.*[30]

Fitspiration does not just impact young women. The magazine *Men's Health* featured an article titled "How #Fitspiration Makes You

Weak." According to the article, social media posts aimed at inspiring men and adolescent males to push through pain to achieve fitness goals had negative impacts on followers. Followers were more likely to harm themselves by pushing their bodies too hard during workouts. Meanwhile, followers of #fitspiration messages that did not have time to go to the gym were more likely to feel low self-esteem, anxiety, and depression.

Fat Bias

In addition to the cultural pressure to embody a particular physique, discrimination against the overweight and obese also fuels dieting in the United States. Writer Elna Baker is one of those rare individuals who lost more than 100 pounds (45 kg) and kept off the weight. She made the decision to lose weight for two reasons: to get a job and to find love. While she had looked for a job for more than a year and a half before her weight loss, she was offered an entry-level position in her field within a month after hitting her goal weight.

Numerous scientific studies corroborate Baker's experience. Overweight and obese individuals are discriminated against throughout the hiring process and on average make $1.25 less per hour. Young women are especially penalized for their weight, with overweight women earning 12 percent less for their work.

From serious economic discrimination to the more commonplace discrimination faced by overweight individuals every day, Baker's story showcases the gulf between life as an overweight young woman in New York City and the privilege granted to those who are thin. After losing weight, Baker began to date someone living in her apartment building, a kindergarten teacher who left love notes on her door. She soon realized that despite knowing him for four years he believed they met for the first time after her weight loss. At her previous weight

BODY SHAMING

Ragini Nag Rao is the curator of the plus-size fashion blog *A Curious Fancy*. In 2014, she wrote for online teen magazine *Rookie* about how body shaming led her deep into an eating disorder. In middle school, she was stronger than the boys and loved the energy that playing sports gave her. But when she dreamed of swimming like the competitors she saw on television, her parents told her she was too fat and she'd look ridiculous. As she internalized these messages, Rao developed an eating disorder, telling herself, "I'm a freak, I'm monstrous. Girls aren't supposed to be 'strong'; girls are *feminine*. I need to be smaller . . ." At age eighteen, after beginning a path toward health, Rao went swimming for the first time. She reconsidered the shame she felt at her own strength. She writes, "Your body is *your* instrument—and you get to use it to do whatever you want. Don't diminish or reshape or neglect it for anyone else. Silence shamers by showing them what you're capable of. Leave them all behind. What they tried to shame you for, take pride in. Your moment has arrived."

Ragini Nag Rao, "Too Fat to Swim: A Cautionary Tale About Letting Other People's Opinions Shrink You Down," *Rookie*, October 16, 2014. www.rookiemag.com.

she had been invisible. Another casually painful incident occurred on a date with a man who told her, "I just can't tolerate fat people."[31]

A moral fury at fatness is nothing new. A 1914 article in the magazine *Living Age* stated, "Fat is now regarded as an indiscretion and almost a crime."[32] Numerous weight-loss programs include a religious element, including the work of Paul Brynteson at Oral Roberts University in the early 1970s. Under Brynteson's direction, the religious school took on the mind, spirit, and body as realms of instruction. The British Broadcasting Corporation documented one faculty member's religious lesson on the condition of being overweight. As the faculty member said, ". . . all things work together for good to those that love God, who are called according to His purpose. Now, my goodness, how can anything like fat be good? And how can God have purpose in a person being fat?"[33]

Since the 1970s, the number of overweight individuals has greatly increased. Paul Campos, a law professor at the University of Colorado, observes that the contemporary "'war on fat' is unique in American history in that it represents the first concerted attempt to transform the vast majority of the nation's citizens into social pariahs, to be pitied and scorned."[34]

Historian Peter Stearns goes so far as to say that the French have had greater success with weight loss than Americans because weight loss in France does not contain the moral element seen in American culture. In the United States, according to Stearns, "[i]f you fail to lose weight you are demonstrating you're a bad person. It's a big burden."[35] Given everything now known about metabolism, leptin, and the functions that truly govern people's weight, it is also a nearly impossible one.

FACTORS CORRELATED WITH DIETING AND DISORDERED EATING IN TEENAGERS

INDIVIDUAL FACTORS
- Overweight and obesity
- Body dissatisfaction
- Low self-esteem
- Low sense of control over life
- Depression and anxiety
- Early puberty

FAMILY FACTORS
- Poor family connection
- Lack of positive adult role models
- Parents who diet
- Parents who encourage dieting
- Parents who criticize their child's weight

ENVIRONMENTAL INFLUENCES
- Weight-related teasing or bullying
- Low involvement in school
- Peer group that encourages dieting
- Involvement in weight-related sports

Canadian Paediatric Society, "Dieting in Adolescence," *Paediatric & Child Health*, September 2004. www.ncbi.nlm.nih.gov.

WHAT ARE THE OUTCOMES OF TEEN DIETING?

Dieting as a teen can have lasting health impacts. Many popular diets have negative health consequences that can be devastating to growing bodies. As Aliya experienced, the Atkins diet can throw the body into ketosis. For many people, ketosis is not stressful for the body, but in some individuals the process can have negative health consequences. Atkins is an example of a rigid diet that is not healthy for all individuals.

Another rigid diet made popular recently is juicing. Juicing involves drinking a variety of juiced fruits and vegetables without the pulp. Most juicing diets strictly restrict calories and require people to avoid eating other food. Nutritionists caution that juicing may not meet all of the body's nutritional needs. Juices often do not contain the fiber found within whole fruit. They often do not include protein, which maintains muscle and supports tissue repair. Unless dark greens are added, juices do not include iron, a micronutrient crucial for energy levels. Extreme diets like juicing can result in malnutrition, which can limit growth in teens and have lasting consequences. Additionally, most juicing diets are only meant to last for a few days. Any weight lost during those few days is likely to be gained back as the dieter returns to his or her regular eating patterns.

Numerous pills and supplements advertise themselves as the quick fix for lowering weight or achieving a more muscular build. These supplements can pose serious health risks and have little scientific evidence to support their claims. Anyone considering a supplement should discuss it with a primary care physician first.

Disordered Eating

In addition to increasing weight gain over time and causing physiological risks related to specific diets, dieting can also cause people to develop unhealthy relationships with food and body image. For many people, dieting is a way to manage stress and negative emotions. Dieting and other disordered eating may allow them to exercise control over their bodies, but it is also often the first step toward developing an eating disorder.

Disordered eating includes any preoccupation with food that is not based on a person's allergies or dietary restrictions. Obsessive concern about "clean" eating falls in this category.

Rogers Behavioral Health describes disordered eating as "an unhealthy relationship with food."[36] When people change their eating habits in response to stressful events, they are engaging in disordered eating. Food shaming can also contribute to disordered eating, and food shaming is a phenomenon increasingly found in everyday language in the United States. Sometimes food shaming is directed toward others. For instance, when someone teases a friend for eating an extra slice of pizza or tells him he needs to go to the gym to work it off, that is food shaming. Food shaming can also be directed toward the self. When a person feels bad for eating that extra slice of pizza, or judges herself for the donut eaten at breakfast, that is also food shaming.

Other warning signs of disordered eating include paying detailed attention to the amount of food eaten, obsessing over "clean" eating, and having strict rules around food. People displaying early signs of disordered eating may cook for others but refuse to eat the food they prepared. Having a consistent reason not to eat, such as "I just ate," "I'm not hungry," or "I'm feeling nauseous," is another indication that an individual could be struggling with disordered eating.

In teenagers, the line between dieting and disordered eating is dangerously thin. The Canadian Pediatric Society states, "changes [from dieting] are often temporary and . . . dieting is unlikely to be effective at achieving sustained weight loss. The majority of teenagers who diet . . . may be putting themselves at risk of consequences with little chance of tangible benefit."[37] The Society considers the negative consequences of teen dieting, such as disordered eating, to outweigh the minimal positive outcomes of dieting.

Disordered eating does not always lead to an eating disorder. But approximately 35 percent of dieters become obsessive dieters, and 20 to 25 percent of those individuals develop eating disorders. Extreme attention to caloric intake, inches on a waistline, and numbers on a bathroom scale can lead to life-threatening illnesses.

Clinical Eating Disorders

Major eating disorders such as anorexia, binge eating disorder, and bulimia receive the most media attention. But the National Eating Disorder Association (NEDA) categorizes several other types of eating disorders. They include extreme restriction of calories, cycles of binging and purging, and obsession with "healthful" eating. NEDA also includes the general category of "unspecified feeding or eating disorder" for when characteristics of an eating disorder cause clinically significant impairment to daily function but do not meet the full criteria of an eating disorder.

Diseases such as anorexia, binge eating disorder, and bulimia can happen to anyone of any gender, size, or background. Eating disorders also affect different ethnic groups at similar rates. However, NEDA cautions, "People of color with self-acknowledged eating and weight concerns were significantly less likely than white participants to have been asked by a doctor about eating disorder symptoms."[38] Eating disorders are complex and dangerous diseases, but they are also possible to overcome with medical support.

Anorexia Nervosa

Anorexia nervosa is the third most common chronic disease among young people, after asthma and type 1 diabetes. NEDA defines anorexia as an eating disorder characterized by weight loss; difficulties maintaining an appropriate body weight for height, age, and stature; and, in many individuals, distorted body image. In some cases with children, anorexia does not actually result in weight loss, but instead prevents people from gaining weight as part of the normal growth process. Individuals struggling with anorexia restrict how many calories they take in and may also use purging behavior or excessive exercise to further prevent weight gain.

There are numerous neurological impacts of anorexia. The brain uses one-fifth of the body's calories, so restricting caloric intake can have a negative impact on brain function and even result in loss of brain matter. People may obsess about food and have trouble concentrating. Disrupted sleep from hunger can affect attention, decision-making, and memory-formation. It can also lead to increased anxiety and depression.

Without a normal intake of food, the levels of minerals in the body drop. Important minerals such as potassium, sodium, chloride, and calcium help promote the functioning of the brain and the signaling that takes place between the brain and the body. Without normal levels of minerals, the electrical and chemical signals in the brain and the body are disrupted. This can lead to seizures and muscle cramps.

With lowered intake of fat and cholesterol, hormone functions in the body can also be thrown into disarray. Menstruation in young women can cease, leading to bone loss and a greater risk of broken bones. Hormone levels are thrown off-balance, and the thyroid cannot properly manage the body's metabolism. Dry skin and hair loss can follow, along with a condition known as *lanugo* in which the body grows fine, downy hair to conserve warmth during periods of starvation.

As the body attempts to continue functioning without enough calories, it will turn to its own muscle. The body breaks down muscles such as the heart for fuel. As the weakened heart attempts to push blood through the body, dangerously low heart rates and blood

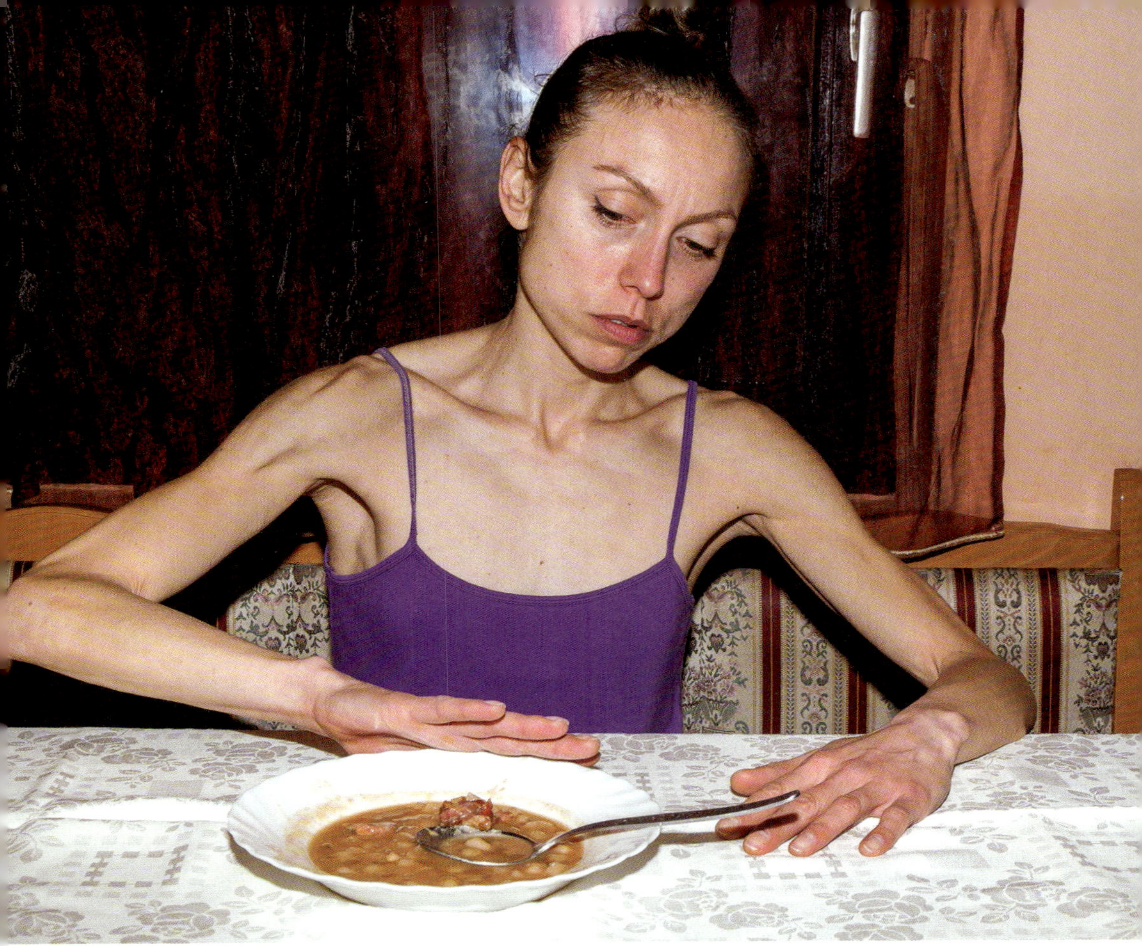

For many who suffer from eating disorders, the goal of thinness is an elusive one. Distorted body image prevents people with anorexia from recognizing when their weight takes an unhealthy turn.

pressure follow. Loss of life is not uncommon with the disease, especially if it is left untreated. Anorexia nervosa is the most frequently fatal psychiatric illness, surpassing even major depressive disorder.

Anorexia is not a new disease. In fourteenth-century Italy, Catherine of Siena was famous for extreme fasting. Writing by Catherine's contemporaries demonstrates how many women's lives were structured around an avoidance of food in order to satisfy, in their eyes, a higher spiritual hunger. In the nineteenth century, such disruption to routine life was given the name anorexia nervosa. Understanding of the disease continued to evolve as the motivation for caloric restriction changed from a standard of character to a standard of physical beauty.

Megan Jayne Crabbe was diagnosed with anorexia at age fourteen. Though anorexia can impact people of all ages and genders, her first memories of wanting to change her body came when she was five years old. Entering school, she began to compare herself to her female classmates. It took Megan two years, intense residential treatment, a hospitalization, and, in her words, "countless tears from the family member's hearts I'd broken along the way" to restore her weight from 65 pounds (29 kg) to a healthy weight.[39]

Her popular blog, *BodyPosiPanda*, is now a source of inspiration and positivity for people struggling with body image and body dissatisfaction. As Megan wrote in 2015, "However you feel about your body right now, please believe that it can get better. You can learn to love every part of yourself, without changing a thing." She went on to say, "Take it from someone who never thought they'd find a way out, there is hope, and happiness, and freedom on the other side of self hatred."[40]

Seamus Kirst lived with anorexia and bulimia throughout high school and college. He wrote about his experience in *Teen Vogue*, saying, "My daily routines were shaped by my obsession with and rejection of food. My moods were dependent on the numbers on a scale, on the visibility of bones protruding through skin."[41] Despite how much his eating disorder affected his life, Seamus struggled to reach out for help with his illness because of the stereotypes around anorexia and the people it affected. "Eating disorders were closely – if not exclusively – thought to be associated with high-achieving, affluent, white teenage girls."[42] Anorexia nervosa will affect an estimated 10 million men each year.

Stereotypes around eating disorders assert that only girls and women experience them. As a result, boys and young men suffering from eating disorders face additional stigma around their symptoms.

NEDA provides extensive resources for those who are experiencing anorexia or who are concerned about a friend or family member. The organization includes lists of physical symptoms and warning signs for the disease. Extreme weight loss is just one of many signs that a person may have anorexia. Other warning signs for the disease include if a person dresses in layers to hide weight loss or to stay warm, or if he or she makes frequent comments about feeling fat or overweight despite losing weight. People with anorexia are often preoccupied with weight, food, calories, fat grams, and dieting. They might also have strict food rules or rituals such as excessive chewing, eating foods in a certain order, or rearranging food on a plate. Finally, obsession over exercise and withdrawal from family and friends are other concerning behaviors linked to anorexia.

Anorexia is a very serious illness that requires specialized intensive treatments, but it is possible for those with the disease to live a long, full, and happy life in recovery. NEDA is just one organization among many that support those seeking recovery.

Bulimia Nervosa

Bulimia nervosa is a disease characterized by cycles of binge eating followed by compensatory behaviors such as self-induced vomiting, excessive exercise, or abuse of laxatives. Bulimia often co-occurs with self-injury, substance abuse, and impulsivity. Bulimia can impact individuals at many weights and all genders, ethnicities, and ages.

Because bulimia includes both periods of binging and starvation, the physiological impacts of the disorder include those present for anorexia and binge eating disorder. Forced purging can deplete electrolytes, minerals that are dissolved in the body's fluids. Having low electrolytes can cause chemical imbalances that harm the heart and affect muscle contraction, leading to spasms and seizures. These chemical imbalances can lead to irregular heartbeats, heart failure, and death.

Forced vomiting interferes with the body's ability to digest nutrients and can lead to stomach pain and bloating, nausea, blood sugar fluctuations, blocked intestines, bacterial infections, and constipation. Forced vomiting can also wear down the esophagus and ultimately cause a life-threatening event if the esophagus ruptures. Purging can cause an inflammation of the pancreas and swelling in the salivary gland. Even a short period of bulimia can have long-term health consequences.

Actress Jane Fonda discussed her struggle with bulimia in her memoir, *Prime Time*. She wrote, "Like many girls, I first began to experience anxiety and depression during adolescence. That is also when my twenty-year-long battle with anorexia and bulimia began." In the book, Fonda describes her eating disorder as "a pattern of disembodiment."[43]

Feeling disconnected with the body is an experience closely connected to bulimia nervosa. Joselyn, a woman interviewed in Becky W. Thompson's book *A Hunger So Wide and So Deep*, spoke poignantly about the disconnect she felt with her body during the depths of her eating disorder: "I have never had a picture of what I look like. I could dream but I could never dream about myself. I could never see myself. . . . I was always just like ashes thrown up in the air, just no shape at all."[44] Many factors can influence this disconnection, including genetic predisposition to depression and eating disorders, cultural pressure, and a history of trauma.

Bulimia nervosa disproportionally affects people of color. Black teenagers are twice as likely to exhibit bulimic behavior as white teenagers, and Hispanic teens are significantly more likely than their non-Hispanic counterparts to suffer from the disease. However, stigma surrounding eating disorders influences the care that teenagers of color receive around eating disorders. In one study, researchers presented clinicians with identical case studies demonstrating disordered eating symptoms in white, Hispanic, and black women. Clinicians were asked to identify if the woman's eating behavior was problematic. Forty-four percent of clinicians identified the white woman's behavior as problematic. Forty-one percent identified the Hispanic woman's behavior as problematic. Only 17 percent identified the black woman's behavior as problematic. The clinicians were also less likely to recommend that the black woman should receive professional help. Though unfair, this research reinforces the importance of individuals advocating for their own health care if clinicians seem hesitant to assist with treatment.

Warning signs of bulimia include weight loss, dieting, and obsession with food. A person with bulimia might show signs of their binge eating and purging by making frequent trips to the bathroom after meals, using laxatives, using excessive amounts of mouth wash and gum to hide the smell from vomiting, and drinking excessive amounts of water to make vomiting easier. Other examples of purging include fasting, excessive exercise, and abuse of medications. Emotional signs of the disease include mood fluctuations and poor self-esteem.

Recovery from bulimia is possible with proper medical support. Eating disorders are serious, but they are also common and treatable. Eating disorders develop and worsen over time. Knowing their warning signs and interrupting their development early on can prevent serious health consequences and lead to a positive relationship with food and body image.

Binge Eating Disorder

Binge eating disorder (BED) is the most common eating disorder in the United States. It is more common than diseases such as breast cancer, HIV/AIDs, and schizophrenia. BED is characterized by chronic feelings of loss of control during eating. These feelings lead to shame, distress, guilt, and the consumption of large amounts of food.

A SOLUTION TO BINGE EATING DISORDER

Dr. Christopher G. Fairburn works at the Centre for Research on Eating Disorders at Oxford University. He has developed an effective method of treating binge eating disorder. The method was first published in 1995 in his book *Overcoming Binge Eating*. One key component of Fairburn's solution to binge eating disorder is for people to quit dieting. He specifically counsels people with BED to resist calorie counting and limiting how much they eat and to stop avoiding particular foods. His treatment program has been studied extensively in clinical trials and has been shown to be very effective in treating BED. Individuals with BED can follow the program on their own or seek the help of a professional as they work through the treatment program outlined in the book. Dr. Fairburn has since published a second edition of his book in 2013 and developed an online version of his material. The online treatment program aims at helping people in the early stages of an eating disorder or those with an established eating disorder that are unable or unwilling to address their illness with face-to-face treatment.

Dieting and binge eating disorder are deeply linked. Three out of ten individuals looking for weight loss treatments such as dieting have BED. Not only is dieting a frequent symptom of individuals already suffering from BED, but caloric restriction from dieting easily leads to BED when a person who has been deprived of food eats more than would be typical or healthy after fasting. This can set off cycles of dieting and binging that have severe negative health consequences for a person's physical and emotional state.

Individuals at all weights can be diagnosed with BED, though the majority of people living with obesity do not have BED. The physical health outcomes of BED include high blood pressure, high cholesterol, heart disease, type 2 diabetes, and gallbladder disease. Binging can also cause a life-threatening rupture to the stomach.

Writer Roxane Gay shares of her experience with BED in her memoir, *Hunger*. She begins by describing the pleasure of eating rich, processed foods with abandon and notes that this was the only true pleasure she received during her adolescence. She writes, "I was swallowing my secrets and making my body expand and explode. I found ways to hide in plain sight, to keep feeding a hunger that could never be satisfied—the hunger to stop hurting. . . . I created a distinct boundary between myself and anyone who dared approach me. I created a boundary between myself and my family."[45]

BED affects men and women almost equally. Ron Saxen is a former male model who struggled with binge eating throughout his life after developing the disease as a teenager. He chronicled his story with NEDA and in his memoir, *The Good Eater: The True Story of One Man's Struggle with Binge Eating Disorder*. In an article for NEDA, he wrote, "To the world I probably seemed like a pretty cool dude . . . someone who had it all figured out. But I didn't. I was a mess. I had an eating disorder that dominated my life, something I kept as hidden as humanly possible."[46]

The *Diagnostic and Statistical Manual of Mental Disorders* only formally recognized BED as a unique eating disorder in 2013 in its fifth edition. It is possible that additional research will show more health complications associated with the condition, but its impact on the lives of individuals struggling with the disorder are clear. People with BED experience difficulties in functioning at work and

"To the world I probably seemed like a pretty cool dude. . . . I was a mess. I had an eating disorder that dominated my life, something I kept as hidden as humanly possible."[46]

– Ron Saxen, former model and sufferer of binge eating disorder social functions, withdrawal from friends and family, and extreme concern with body shape and size. They exhibit an obsession with fad diets and frequent dieting. Depression, anxiety, and feelings of overwhelming shame are a few of the emotional and psychological outcomes of BED.

Less than half of the individuals living with BED seek treatment, but it is possible to receive psychological, medical, and behavioral treatments and live in recovery from BED. NEDA and other organizations provide resources for supporting individuals with the disease and their friends and family.

Treating Eating Disorders

Treatment for an eating disorder often begins with residential care, in which teenagers live in a facility and have a team of doctors, psychologists, and nutritionists on hand to support their recovery. Individual and group therapy helps teens address the psychological and emotional causes of disordered eating and eating disorders, including low self-esteem, poor body image, and shame. Group therapy in particular helps teens see that they are not alone in their struggles. Doctors and nutritionists monitor teens' physical health and ensure they are receiving the proper nutrition they need. Nutritionists also help educate teens about food and healthy eating. In time, teens transition to outpatient programs so they can continue to receive support as they recover from disordered eating or eating disorders.

Through their treatment, teens learn skills for healthy eating and healthy living, including practices such as mindful eating. These skills can benefit teens without a diagnosed eating disorder. Anyone who experiences disordered eating or who struggles with body image and self-esteem can learn to break the cycle of dieting and body dissatisfaction.

Chapter 4

HOW CAN TEENS BREAK THE CYCLE OF DIETING?

In the United States, roughly half of the population will try a diet each year, including, by some reports, half of all teenage girls. Dieting becomes cyclical. When the first diet fails, perhaps even resulting in weight gain, people often try a new dieting program. The more people repress their hunger, the more they disturb their natural metabolism. This makes it more difficult for the body to effectively communicate feelings of hunger and fullness. After a person begins dieting, following strict rules for eating can be the only way for them to regulate food intake because natural communication within the body is so disrupted.

How does the cycle of dieting end? Research suggests long-term lifestyle changes can lead to a healthy weight, a positive relationship with food, and improved overall health.

Intuitive Eating

A study published in 2005 looked closely at two groups of young women in San Francisco, California, who were considered medically obese. The study was interested in weight, BMI, blood pressure, cholesterol, energy expenditure, eating behavior, and psychological health. During a six-month period, half of the group went on a diet and half of the group went on a "health at every size" program. Researchers describe this program as emphasizing intuitive eating, or eating "in response to internal cues of hunger, satiety, and appetite."[47]

After one year from the start of the study, the diet group was shown to have lost weight. After two years, the diet group had regained the weight and showed no lasting positive impact in the various measures of health. Meanwhile, the women in the intuitive eating program maintained their weight but improved in all other health areas. The study showed intuitive eating and focusing on health at every size allowed individuals to maintain long-term positive changes in their health.

A further study at the University of Minnesota surveyed 2,287 young adults about their BMI and whether they trusted their bodies to tell them when they were full. Rates of intuitive eating correlated with lower BMI. Teens who trust cues of hunger and fullness are less likely to be overweight than those who do not follow intuitive eating signals.

Intuitive eating is not dieting. It is the idea that following hunger signals is the most effective way to manage eating. Diets often propagate the idea that a single method of eating is the best way for every body. Intuitive eating emphasizes the body's innate ability to seek and take in the nutrition it needs. The body self-regulates through complex hormonal cues that manage feelings of hunger and satisfaction.

Intuitive eating is also called non-dieting, or the non-diet approach. It is a common tool used to treat both obesity and eating disorders in individuals of all ages. Dr. Evelyn Tribole and nutritionist Elyse Resch give several guidelines for intuitive eating.

Dieting requires people to ignore their hunger. Binge eating often occurs after a sustained period of caloric restriction, which is to say an individual ignores mild and moderate hunger cues until the need becomes overwhelming. Instead of cycling between starving and binging, Tribole and Resch argue that dieters should "honor [their] hunger."[48] After extensive dieting, it can take a long time to reestablish natural hunger cues. But listening for small cues of hunger and staying fed throughout the day builds awareness of eating signals and keeps the body properly nourished.

Dieters tend to have black-and-white thinking around food. Intuitive eating requires people to let go of hard and fast rules around food. In her book *Brave Girl Eating: A Family's Struggle with Anorexia*, writer Harriet Brown begins with a description of a young woman standing in front of a bakery in Paris and looking into a window filled with croissants, petit fours, and crusty baguettes. She writes, "You can almost taste the bread she's eating. Almost. But you can't, not really, because how long has it been since you've tasted bread?"[49] Disordered eating can stem from people categorizing certain foods as "good" and certain foods as "bad." This food shaming can be internalized. The moral categories used to describe food are then used to describe the people themselves, such that those who eat certain foods feel bad themselves. The rigidity of these beliefs makes recovery from an eating disorder and recovery from dieting a long and difficult process.

For many individuals, eating too much or too little food is an unhealthy tool for managing stress. Intuitive eating suggests that people can find other healthy ways to honor their feelings, deal with stress, and experience pleasure—without using food. Because food can be comforting, denial of that comfort or overindulging in that comfort can seem productive. However, food cannot actually fix a problem. It cannot even successfully manage weight loss. Developing other tools for managing stress can help ease the unhealthy pressure around eating. Group activities such as sports or dance, learning a new skill such as playing an instrument or drawing, and even playing with a loved pet are all healthy activities that can take the place of dieting or excessive eating.

Intuitive eating also encourages people to respect their bodies. Body positivity involves appreciating the unique body every individual is born with. It is difficult for people to maintain physical health and take care of their bodies if they feel a great deal of hatred toward the way their bodies look. Health and body acceptance are deeply connected. Body acceptance has been shown to reduce abuse

COSMETIC SURGERY

Writer Katie McMahon had liposuction, a procedure to surgically remove fat from her body, when she was eighteen years old. "While many people choose to have cosmetic surgery for their own totally valid reasons, my reasons were based in shame," she wrote in the online magazine *Rookie*. "I hated my body, and I had surgery to get rid of it and replace it with one that wouldn't embarrass me." Much of Katie's shame came from her mother. Katie's mother put her on a diet when she was eleven, signed Katie up for sports she did not want to play, and led Katie to binge eating when she was fourteen. Katie's mother began bringing up liposuction when Katie was sixteen. Even after the procedure, Katie still felt fat.

It took a college acting class for Katie to consider changing the relationship she had with her body. "I decided to make peace with my body. The first step was to catch myself whenever I started an internal stream of negative commentary about my shape, my weight, my personality, my value." When Katie exercises now, it is to feel good and not to lose weight. As she wrote in her post, "It helps me remember that my body's got more important things to do than maintain some unrealistic physical label. This is what progress looks like for me."

Katie McMahon, "Out of (My) Body: I Totally Wanted Liposuction—Until I Got It," *Rookie*, March 25, 2014. www.rookiemag.com.

of alcohol and cigarettes and has many positive impacts on health
in teenage girls. The social media campaign #bopo allows many
young people of all genders and sizes to express body positivity and
size acceptance.

A final component of intuitive
eating is to learn to recognize
feelings of fullness. The body
signals the brain when enough
food has been eaten. Pausing
while eating gives these signals
time to reach the brain. Thinking
through the taste of food or current levels of fullness can help reinforce
these cues. Mindful eating is another tool people can use to reinforce
these signals.

Mindful Eating

If intuitive eating is about cues of hunger and fullness from the
body, mindful eating is about fully experiencing every meal, rather
than dwelling on the emotional implications that can often lead to
disordered eating. Mindful eating can help reinforce cues around
intuitive eating.

The Center for Mindful Eating, a nonprofit focused on providing
education for professionals and individuals around mindful eating,
provides guidelines for developing a balanced, respectful, healthy, and
joyful relationship with food by combining principles of mindfulness
and healthy eating. The center offers the following description
of mindfulness: "Mindfulness is deliberately paying attention,
non-judgmentally, in the present moment. . . . Mindfulness is being
aware of your thoughts, emotions and physical sensations in the
present moment."[50]

When mindfulness is applied to eating, the result is an eating practice that promotes a healthy relationship to the body and to food. The Center for Mindful Eating describes the practice as "using all your senses in choosing to eat food that is both satisfying to you and nourishing to your body."[51] Mindful eating encourages people to develop their own individual relationships to food.

Research conducted in 2010 at the University of New Mexico and the Oregon Research Institute's Center for Family and Adolescent Research showed that mindful eating had a significant impact on young men considered medically obese. Participants in the study were able to successfully incorporate mindful eating practices and also lower their weight.

Mindful eating does not mean eating silently in a serious meditative state. There are a few simple tools that can bring a simple mindfulness practice to food. First, mindful eating experts recommend setting aside time to eat food instead of including it as part of another event. Often food is included in other activities. People snack during movies, eat dinner while watching TV, or eat a granola bar while running to class. Overeating often occurs because another input—such as from a movie or television show—drowns out the bodily cue of fullness. People do not have to eat alone or in silence. But limiting the amount of time spent eating and doing other activities can prevent overeating.

Second, mindful eating recommends that people pay attention to the first bite of food. The very first bite of food is often the most rewarding. A simple way into mindful eating is to relish that first bite of food or the first sip of something refreshing and delicious. Mindful eating emphasizes the natural enjoyment of food. When each bite is savored, overeating is less rewarding.

A third strategy advanced by mindful eating is to slow down the pace of eating. Many people eat in a hurry, already loading their forks with the next bite before finishing off their current mouthful of food. A simple rule is for people to keep their forks empty when their mouths are full. This practice slows down eating and helps people avoid overeating. It also encourages people to bring more awareness to the process of actually eating every bite.

Another method of engaging mindfully with each bite is to follow a mindful eating script. These scripts can be found online. They act like guided meditations people can follow as they eat a meal. One script begins by directing individuals to bring awareness to sensations in the body before eating. It asks, "If you were going to eat or drink something right now, what is your body hungry for? What is it thirsty for?" The script goes on to encourage individuals to bring their awareness to their meal and to "notice the color, shape, texture, and size" of the food on their plate.[52] Further cues in the script guide the eaters' attention to the physical experience of eating food and invite eaters to feel gratitude for the food they are eating. The intention of the mindful eating script is to make eating a meaningful and intentional act.

Finally, mindful eating suggests that people create a meal-ending ritual. Cues from the body to stop eating are subtle. Oftentimes after a meal the brain is still looking for a little something extra to eat. Building a habit for clearly ending a meal can help reinforce to the brain that the time for eating has ended. Over time, this habit will contribute to feelings of satisfaction after a meal. The ritual itself can be as simple as doing the dishes, brushing teeth, eating a mint, or chewing a piece of gum.

People who focus on healthy eating as part of a larger goal of overall health are often more successful than those who diet strictly to lower weight. Healthy eating involves eating from all five food groups in moderation.

Shared Meals

Increasingly, meals in the United States are a solo experience. The majority of American families eat a family meal together fewer than five days a week. Eating meals together, particularly within a family structure, can have significant positive health and behavioral results.

The Organization for Economic Cooperation and Development found that young people who do not eat dinner with their families at least twice a week are 40 percent more likely to be overweight. This is because meals eaten outside of the home, such as at fast food restaurants and take-out places, tend to be less healthy than the meals made at home. Meanwhile, by eating in a family structure, young people see a model of eating for nourishment. Their chances of developing disordered eating habits decrease.

According to the National Center on Addiction and Substance Abuse at Columbia University, as family dinners increase in frequency, so do academic performance and healthy eating. Meanwhile, issues with drugs and alcohol decrease. Making time to share meals in a family setting can be a lifestyle change that naturally facilitates a healthy weight.

Overall Health

One of the most common reasons people diet is to improve overall health. But focusing only on losing weight can pose serious negative health consequences. Despite the intention of dieting for better health, dieters almost inevitably cause their health to deteriorate.

However, the opposite approach is effective. Focusing on overall health can help bring weight to a healthy level as it improves general mental and physical well-being. Components of overall mental and physical health include physical activity, adequate sleep, and body acceptance.

Physical Activity

Being physically active is essential for good health. An active lifestyle facilitates strong bone, muscle, and joint development and also reduces a range of chronic diseases. According to the World Health Organization, "Physical activity has also been associated with psychological benefits in young people by improving their control over symptoms of anxiety and depression."[53]

For most children and young adults between the ages of six and seventeen, health professionals recommend sixty minutes of activity per day for at least five days a week for a healthy, active lifestyle. Those sixty minutes per day do not have to be at a high intensity, nor do they have to be consecutive. There are many creative ways to stay active. Participating in traditional sports is a great way to stay healthy. Other activities, such as rock climbing, weight lifting, yoga, dance, martial arts, biking, and hiking, are additional examples.

Extreme physical activity or exercise can be dangerous. Compulsive exercising can even be a sign of an eating disorder. Meanwhile, compensatory exercise, or exercising to make up for the food one has eaten, can be a sign of food shaming and disordered eating.

The Health at Every Size movement contrasts these negative forms of exercise with "life-enhancing movement," or "physical activities that allow people of all sizes, abilities, and interests to engage in enjoyable movement, to the degree that they choose."[54] Life-enhancing movement prioritizes movement over exercise by considering the ways in which the body is already in movement and by identifying ways to make movement meaningful and enjoyable.

To further encourage creative methods of movement, author and educator Rochelle Rice recommends writing down a list of the activities that come to mind with each letter of the alphabet. For example, A is for archery, B is for baton twirling, C is for canoeing, etc. People can get involved in these out-of-the-box, creative ways of engaging in movement.

Movement that builds greater body awareness, such as dance, yoga, and martial arts, can be very effective at healing body dysmorphia and disordered eating. A person with body dysmorphia is obsessively preoccupied with flaws in his or her appearance, flaws that are often unnoticeable or very minor to others. Body dysmorphia leads to feelings of shame and anxiety. It most often develops in teens and adolescents, and it affects males and females equally.

Much of the trauma of eating disorders and strict dieting happens when a person's own body becomes a stranger. Susan Kleinman, a dance and movement therapist, writes, "Many individuals with eating disorders describe the experience of being in their bodies as *disembodied*, as if living with a stranger or an enemy."[55] Through mindful activity, the body becomes a strong ally rather than a disorderly force to be reckoned with and controlled through dieting. Several movement practices, such as NIA, Qoya, yoga, and tai chi, specifically aim to restore the connection between the body and the mind.

Sleep

Research has uncovered the dramatic health impact of inadequate sleep. Inadequate sleep more than doubles the risk of developing cancer, impacts the immune system, increases the risk of memory loss and heart disease, disrupts blood sugar, and increases weight by slowing down the metabolism. Not only does sufficient sleep make it easier to remain at a healthy weight, but it also promotes overall health as much as diet and exercise do. Sleep is especially important for teenagers. The National Sleep Foundation states, "Teens need about 8 to 10 hours of sleep each night to function best. Most teens do not get enough sleep—one study found that only 15% reported sleeping 8 ½ hours on school nights."[56]

Body Acceptance

One common myth around dieting says that happiness will be reached at the same time as a person's goal weight. But happiness and self-acceptance can be part of the healthy eating process. According to the 2005 intuitive eating study in San Francisco, they actually help improve overall health. As gradual lifestyle changes are put into place and a healthy weight becomes part of a larger structure of good health, emotional and psychological health must be the pillars holding everything together.

Body positivity activist Jessamyn Stanley encourages her yoga students to focus on how they feel instead of how they look while practicing yoga. This simple switch helps people feel more connected to and accepting of their bodies.

A 2005 study in Turkey surveyed 531 adolescents about their body acceptance. The study found that having a thinner body ideal, low self-worth, and low self-image were the biggest indicators of dieting in both young men and women, much more so than a high BMI. Breaking the cycle of dieting begins with confronting self-image and self-worth.

Body acceptance is the idea that no body is more deserving of love, respect, or dignity than any other. Body positivity does not mean losing weight is bad, but it also does not draw a false equivalence between being thin and being healthy, nor does it put moral classifications on bodies of different sizes or shapes. Body appreciation is a key step toward body acceptance. Body appreciation is the practice of appreciating and feeling gratitude for all the ways people's bodies allow them to move through the world. A body appreciation practice could be as simple as writing down, "I am grateful that my hand moves across a page, allowing me to write this."

Many dieters hope they will achieve happiness after they lose weight. But happiness is possible at every shape and size.

The Journey Toward Health

A key component of health is self-compassion. Self-compassion is the straightforward principle that people should treat themselves the same way they would treat others. Often people speak about their own bodies much more critically than they do anyone else's. Changing that dialogue with the self can have a powerful impact on a person's mental and physical health.

Walt Whitman begins his famous poem "Song of Myself" by saying, "I celebrate myself, and sing myself / And what I assume you shall assume, / For every atom belonging to me as good belongs to you."[57] It is powerful and healthy for people to celebrate the strength and resilience of their bodies, no matter their shape or size. Diet culture insists change must occur before people can live a fulfilled life. The ultimate end to cycles of dieting begins with the understanding that a full and happy life starts right now.

RECOGNIZING SIGNS OF TROUBLE

The Academy for Eating Disorders offers the following early warning signs for an eating disorder:

- Significant weight change or weight fluctuations
- Sudden changes in eating behaviors, including eliminating certain foods
- Sudden changes in exercise patterns, including exercise that is excessive or compulsive
- Any extreme dieting behavior
- Body image disturbance, including the desire to lose weight despite low weight or weight in a normal range
- Pain or aches in the abdominal area
- Problems maintaining electrolytes that have not been linked to a medical cause
- For women and girls, irregular or absent menstruation
- Low blood sugar
- Heart rate below the normal range
- Compensating for eating or binge eating by engaging in purging behaviors, such as vomiting, dieting, fasting, or excessive exercise
- Inappropriate use of nutritional supplements marketed for weight loss

Chapter Three also describes examples and warning signs of disordered eating. While disordered eating does not always lead to an eating disorder or to physical health problems, it is linked to food shaming and body dissatisfaction. Individuals can pay attention to their own eating habits and how those habits contribute to or negatively impact body acceptance and health.

ORGANIZATIONS TO CONTACT

Academy of Nutrition and Dietetics

www.eatright.org

The largest organization of food and nutrition professionals in the world provides research, education, and advocacy on public health and nutrition.

American Nutrition Association

americannutritionassociation.org

This nonprofit provides nutrition education through programs and online information.

Binge Eating Disorder Association

bedaonline.com

BEDA provides education, outreach, and advocacy about binge eating disorder and its diagnosis and treatment.

The Body Positive

www.thebodypositive.org

This organization focuses on helping people to have a more joyful relationship with and reconnect to the wisdom of their bodies.

National Eating Disorders Association

www.nationaleatingdisorders.org

NEDA is a nonprofit that supports individuals affected by eating disorders.

Project HEAL

theprojectheal.org

This organization raises money to help those suffering from eating disorders afford treatment.

SOURCE NOTES

Introduction: The World of Dieting

1. Sandra Aamodt, *Why Diets Make Us Fat: The Unintended Consequences of Our Obsession with Weight Loss*. New York: Current, 2016, p. 2.

2. Crystal Karges, "The Power of Resistance: Saying No to the Diet Culture," *Project HEAL*, May 4, 2017. theprojectheal.org.

3. Megan Jayne Crabbe, "Why I Will Never Bring Diet Talk Into the Body Positive Community," *Bodyposipanda* (blog), November 26, 2015. www.bodyposipanda.com.

4. Joan Jacobs Brumberg, *The Body Project: An Intimate History of American Girls.* New York: Random House, 1997, p. 97.

5. Louise Foxcroft, *Calories and Corsets: A History of Dieting Over 2,000 Years*. London: Profile Books, 2012, p. 2.

6. Andrea Bombak, "Obesity, Health at Every Size, and Public Health Policy," *American Journal of Public Health*, February 2014, pp. 60–67.

Chapter 1: What Is Dieting?

7. Neville H. Golden, Marcie Schneider, and Christine Wood, "Preventing Obesity and Eating Disorders in Adolescents," *American Academy of Pediatrics*, August 2016. pediatrics.aapublications.org.

8. Irving Fisher and Eugene Lyman Fisk, *How to Live: Rules for Healthful Living Based on Modern Science*. New York: Funk and Wagnalls, 1916, p. 33.

9. Quoted in Gina Kolata, *Rethinking Thin: The New Science of Weight Loss—and the Myths and Realities of Dieting*. New York: Picador, 2008, p. 53.

10. Quoted in Megan Fox, "America's Obesity Epidemic Hits a New High," *NBC News,* June 7, 2016. www.nbcnews.com.

11. N. I. Larson, M. T. Story, and M. C. Nelson, "Neighborhood Environments: Disparities in Access to Healthy Foods in the US," *American Journal of Preventative Medicine*, January 2009, pp. 74–81.

12. Kelly D. Brownell, "Culture Matters in the Obesity Debate," *LA Times*, September 21, 2007. www.latimes.com.

13. "Obesity and Overweight: Fact Sheet," *World Health Organization*, October 2017. www.who.int.

14. Sandra Aamodt, *Why Diets Make Us Fat: The Unintended Consequences of Our Obsession with Weight Loss*. New York: Current, 2016, p. 9.

15. Quoted in Andrew J. Hill, "Does Dieting Make You Fat?" *British Journal of Nutrition* 92, August 2004, pp. 15–18.

16. Helen Riess and Mary Dockray-Miller, "Set-Point Theory," *MIT Medical*, n.d. medical.mit.edu.

17. Helen Riess and Mary Dockray-Miller, "Set-Point Theory."

18. "Body Image?" *National Eating Disorders Association*, 2017. www.nationaleatingdisorders.org.

Chapter 2: Why Do Teens Diet?

19. Quoted in Bill Chappell, "Mindy Kaling on Diets, High School and Other American Pastimes," *National Public Radio*, November 1, 2011. www.npr.org.

20. Canadian Paediatric Society, "Dieting in Adolescence," *Paediatrics & Child Health*, September 2004, pp. 487–491.

21. "Body & Beauty Standards," *Bradley University,* 2018. www.bradley.edu.

22. Hillel Schwartz, *Never Satisfied: A Cultural History of Diets, Fantasies and Fat.* New York: Free Press (Macmillan, Inc.), 1986, p. 147.

23. Quoted in Joan Jacobs Brumberg, *The Body Project: An Intimate History of American Girls.* New York: Random House, 1997, p. xxi.

24. Quoted in Joan Jacobs Brumberg, *The Body Project.* p. xxi.

25. Roxane Gay, *Hunger.* New York: Harper Collins, 2017, p. 135.

26. *Time*, February 2016.

27. Quoted in Jamie Santa Cruz, "Body-Image Pressure Increasingly Affects Boys," *Atlantic*, March 10, 2014. www.theatlantic.com.

28. Quoted in Gina Kolata, "After 'The Biggest Loser,' Their Bodies Fought to Regain Weight," *New York Times*, May 2, 2016. www.nytimes.com.

29. M. Tiggemann and M. Zaccardo, "'Exercise to Be Fit, Not Skinny': The Effect of Fitspiration Imagery on Women's Body Image," *Body Image*, September 2015, pp. 61–67.

30. Jennifer Lewallen and Elizabeth Behm-Morawitz, "Pinterest or Thinterest?: Social Comparison and Body Image on Social Media," *Social Media + Society*, March 30, 2016, pp. 1–9.

31. Elna Baker, "It's a Small World After All," *This American Life*, June 17, 2016. www.thisamericanlife.org.

32. Quoted in Dinitia Smith, "Demonizing Fat in the War on Weight," *New York Times,* May 1, 2004. www.nytimes.com.

33. Daniel Engber, "Cross Trainers," *This American Life*, June 17, 2016. www.thisamericanlife.org.

34. Quoted in Dinitia Smith, "Demonizing Fat in the War on Weight."

35. Quoted in Dinitia Smith, "Demonizing Fat in the War on Weight."

Chapter 3: What Are the Outcomes of Teen Dieting?

36. "Disordered Eating vs. Eating Disorders," *Rogers Behavioral Health*, May 9, 2013. rogersbh.org.

37. Canadian Paediatric Society, "Dieting in Adolescence," *Paediatrics & Child Health*, September 2004, pp. 487–491.

38. "People of Color and Eating Disorders," *National Eating Disorder Association*, 2018. www.nationaleatingdisorders.org.

39. Megan Jayne Crabbe, "My Journey to Body Positivity," *BodyPosiPanda* (blog), October 30, 2015. www.bodyposipanda.com.

40. Megan Jayne Crabbe, "My Journey to Body Positivity."

41. Seamus Kirst, "I'm a Guy and I Survived an Eating Disorder, Eating Disorders Happen to Everyone," *Teen Vogue*, March 3, 2017. www.teenvogue.com.

42. Seamus Kirst, "I'm a Guy and I Survived an Eating Disorder."

43. Jane Fonda, *Prime Time*. New York: Random House, 2011, p. 44.

44. Quoted in Becky W. Thompson, *A Hunger So Wide and So Deep*. Minneapolis: University of Minnesota, 1992, p. 50.

45. Roxane Gay, *Hunger*. New York: Harper Collins, 2017, p. 61.

46. Ron Saxen, "Beginning Is How You Get There," *National Eating Disorders Association*, 2018. www.nationaleatingdisorders.org.

Chapter 4: How Can Teens Break the Cycle of Dieting?

47. Linda Bacon, J. S. Stern, M. D. Van Loan, and N. L. Kelm, "Size Acceptance and Intuitive Eating Improve Health for Obese, Female Chronic Dieters," *Journal of the American Dietetic Association*, June 2005, pp. 929–936.

48. "Ten Principles of Intuitive Eating," *IntuitiveEating.org*, 2017. www.intuitiveeating.org.

49. Harriet Brown, *Brave Girl Eating: A Family's Struggle with Anorexia*. New York: Harper Collins, 2010, p. 2.

50. "Principles of Mindful Eating," *Center for Mindful Eating*, 2013. thecenterformindfuleating.org.

51. "Principles of Mindful Eating."

52. Christine Milovani, "A Mindful Eating Script," *Office of Patient Centered Care & Cultural Transformation*, 2016. projects.hsl.wisc.edu.

53. "Physical Activity and Young People," *World Health Organization*, 2018. www.who.int.

54. Rochelle Rice, "The HAES® Files: Creating a Buffet of Movement," *Association for Size Diversity and Health*, May 8, 2014. healthateverysizeblog.org.

55. Susan Kleinman, "The Body Speaks: Dance/Movement Therapy Creates Movement Toward Eating Disorders Recovery," *Eating Disorders Resource Catalogue*, January 3, 2016. www.edcatalogue.com.

56. "Teens and Sleep," *National Sleep Foundation*, 2018. sleepfoundation.org.

57. Walt Whitman, "Song of Myself," *Modern American Poetry*, n.d. www.english.illinois.edu.

FOR FURTHER RESEARCH

BOOKS

Sandra Aamodt, *Why Diets Make Us Fat: The Unintended Consequences of Our Obsession with Weight Loss*. New York: Current, 2016.

Jan Chozen Bays. *Mindful Eating: A Guide to Rediscovering a Healthy and Joyful Relationship with Food*. Boulder, CO: Shambhala, 2017.

Carolyn Costin, *The Eating Disorder Sourcebook: A Comprehensive Guide to the Causes, Treatments, and Prevention of Eating Disorders*. New York: McGraw-Hill, 2007.

Megan Jayne Crabbe, *Body Positive Power: Because Life Is Already Happening and You Don't Need Flat Abs to Live It*. New York: Seal Press, 2018.

Kimberly Rae Miller, *Beautiful Bodies: A Memoir*. New York: Little A, 2017.

Jessamyn Stanley, *Every Body Yoga: Let Go of Fear, Get on the Mat, Love Your Body*. New York: Workman, 2017.

Evelyn Tribole and Elyse Resch, *The Intuitive Eating Workbook: Principles for Nourishing a Healthy Relationship with Food*. Oakland, CA: New Harbinger Publications, 2017.

INTERNET SOURCES

Canadian Paediatric Society, "Dieting in Adolescence," *Paediatric & Child Health*, September 2004. www.ncbi.nlm.nih.gov.

Dianne Neumark-Sztainer, Melanie Wall, Nicole I. Larson, Marla E. Eisenberg, and Katie Loth, "Dieting and Disordered Eating Behaviors from Adolescence to Young Adulthood: Findings from a 10-Year Longitudinal Study," *Journal of the American Dietetic Association*, July 2011. www.ncbi.nlm.nih.gov.

National Institute of Diabetes and Digestive and Kidney Diseases, "Take Charge of Your Health: A Guide for Teenagers," *National Institute of Health*, December 2016. www.niddk.nih.gov.

Paediatric & Child Health, "Dieting: Information for Teens," *Paediatric & Child Health*, September 2004. www.ncbi.nlm.nih.gov.

WEBSITES

Association for Size Diversity and Health

www.sizediversityandhealth.org

This nonprofit is an international organization committed to the Health at Every Size principles. It promotes health and wellness education and research that is free from weight discrimination.

BodyPosiPanda

www.bodyposipanda.com

Megan Jayne Crabbe's blog is a resource for teens on topics ranging from diet culture and recovery to self-love and body positivity.

Health at Every Size

www.haescommunity.com

The Health at Every Size community provides resources for those seeking to learn more about the movement.

INDEX

ABOUT THE AUTHOR

Anjali Stenquist lives in Minneapolis, Minnesota. She received her BA from Wellesley College and a Masters in Fine Arts from the University of Wisconsin-Madison.